This book belongs to:

MAQIVE 2005

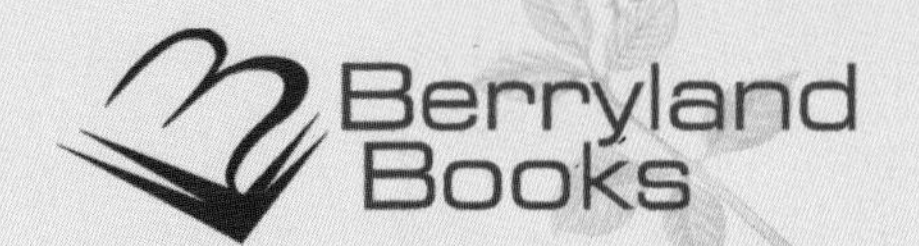

Written by Gill Davies
Illustrated by Eric Kincaid
Edited by Heather Maddock

Published by Berryland Books
www.berrylandbooks.com

First published in 2004

ISBN 1-84577-007-2
Printed in India

Sleeping Beauty

Reading should always be FUN!

Reading is one of the most important skills your child will learn. It's an exciting challenge that you can enjoy together.

Treasured Tales is a collection of stories that has been carefully written for young readers.

Here are some useful points to help you teach your child to read.

Try to set aside a regular quiet time for reading at least three times a week.

Choose a time of the day when your child is not too tired.

Plan to spend approximately 15 minutes on each session.

Select the book together and spend the first few minutes talking about the title and cover picture.

Spend the next ten minutes listening and encouraging your child to read.

Always allow your child to look at and use the pictures to help them with the story.

Spend the last couple of minutes asking your child about what they have read. You will find a few examples of questions at the bottom of some pages.

Understanding what they have read is as important as the reading itself.

Once upon a time, in a far away land, a beautiful Princess was born.

The King and Queen were so happy. They wanted to have a big party to celebrate.

"We shall invite all of our friends and we must ask the seven good fairies to be her godmothers," said the Queen.

The King agreed and the invitations were sent out.

How many godmothers will the Princess have?

The Princess' special day arrived and all the guests came.

One by one the seven good fairies stepped forward to grant their wishes to the Princess.

"She shall be as beautiful as the flowers in Spring," said the first fairy.

The second fairy wished that the Princess would be full of music.

The third fairy wished that she would be as rich as gold.

The next three fairies stepped forward to grant their wishes.

"She shall be as sweet as Summer fruit," said the fourth.

"She shall be as wise as the wisest owl," said the fifth.

"She shall be as happy as a babbling brook," said the sixth.

Suddenly, a very angry fairy pushed her way through.

"You have forgotten me!" she screeched.

"You did not ask me to come and now I shall cast a spell!"

This was the wicked fairy from the north and the King and Queen were afraid of her evil powers.

Why didn't the King and Queen ask the wicked fairy to come?

"The Princess will prick her finger on her sixteenth birthday and she will die!" the wicked fairy screamed.

Then she turned around and left the room, shouting, "You will never forget me again!"

The seventh good fairy stepped forward to grant her wish.

She said she could change the evil wish of the wicked fairy.

"I promise that the Princess will not die but will fall into a deep sleep for one hundred years."

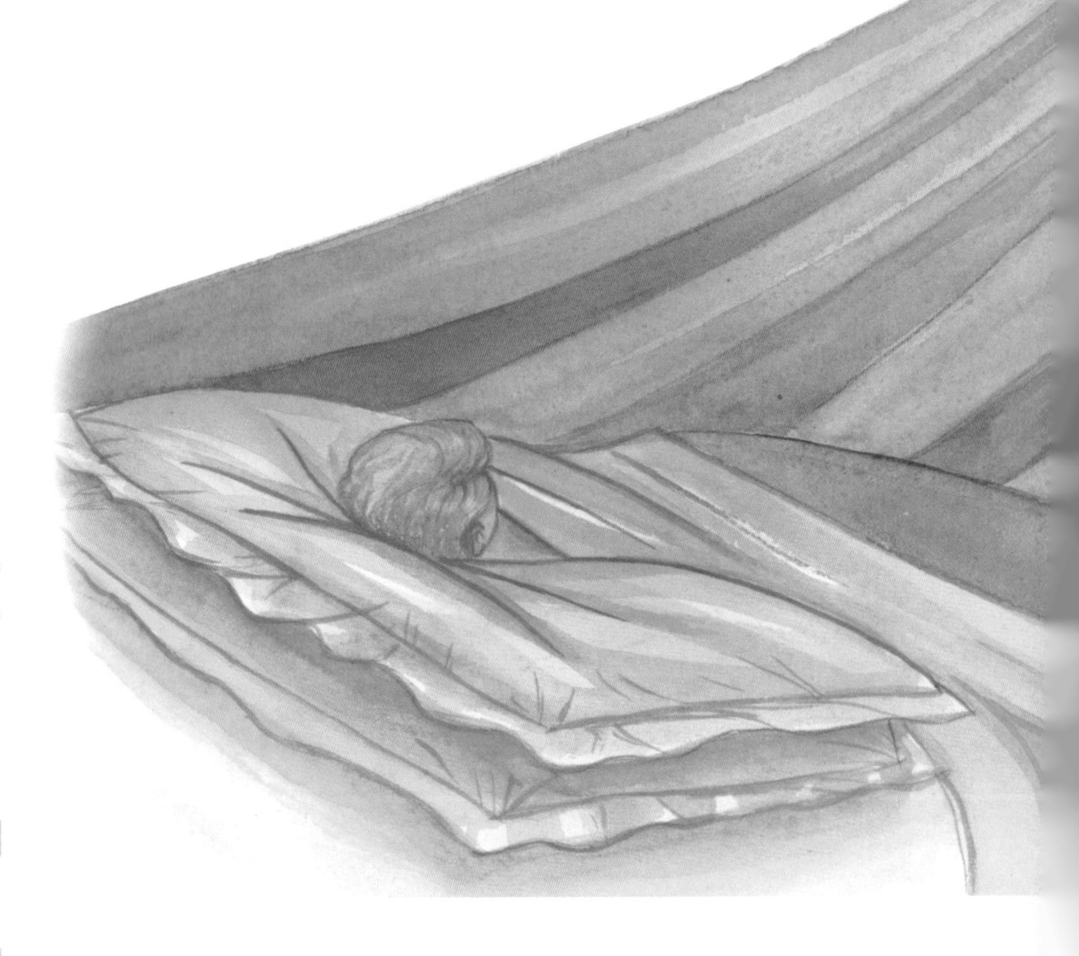

How long will the Princess sleep for?

Time passed and all the good fairies' wishes came true.

The Princess was beautiful, sweet, happy and very clever.

As her sixteenth birthday approached, the King and Queen remembered the words of the wicked fairy.

All the spinning wheels and needles in the palace were thrown away.

Why were the spinning wheels and needles thrown away?

On the day of her birthday, the King and Queen gave the Princess a wonderful party.

She wore a beautiful golden dress that sparkled as she danced.

Suddenly, the Princess felt hot and went outside for some fresh air.

There she saw a bright light shining from a tall tower which she had never seen before.

The Princess wanted to see who was there and so she climbed up the tower.

At the top of the tower, she found an old lady sitting at a spinning wheel.

She reached out to touch the wheel and pricked her finger.

At once, she fell to the floor and into a deep sleep.

The wicked fairy jumped up, laughing, and flew away into the dark sky.

Then the good fairy appeared and cast a magic spell so that everyone else fell fast asleep too.

Years went by and the gardens around the palace grew into a thick forest.

No one could find their way through.

Soon the palace was hidden.

The Princess became known as Sleeping Beauty.

Why did everyone call her Sleeping Beauty?

One day a handsome Prince who lived far away heard the story of Sleeping Beauty.

He was a brave Prince and he wanted to go and see if he could find her.

He climbed onto his horse and set off
on his great adventure.

It took a long time to reach the palace.

When he arrived it was one hundred years after Sleeping Beauty had fallen asleep.

As the Prince started to cut his way through the forest a magical wind began to blow.

The wind was sent by the seventh good fairy and slowly the forest began to disappear.

Soon the Prince was able to ride up to the gates and he walked inside.

He saw a light coming from the tower and started to climb to the top.

There he found Sleeping Beauty and bent down to kiss her.

What do you think happens next?

The magic spell was broken.

Sleeping Beauty and everyone in the palace woke up.

The Prince and Princess fell in love.

They married the very next day and, of course, lived happily ever after.